To John, Thank You.

First Edition

When Timmy starts daydreaming on his boogie board, he drifts far out to sea and is rescued by a friendly octopus, named Rex. To thank Rex, Timmy agrees to take Rex around land, putting Rex's life in danger.

Eight Legs Publishing

Book design by Andrew Baron

ISBN 0-976-034-803
Printed in Korea

The Adventures of Octopus Rex

Written by Barbara Hart
Illustrations by Andrew Baron
Narrated by C.C. Couch
Audio Production by Teddy Irwin

"Don't go out too far," yelled Timmy's mom. "Stay close to the shore."

"Ok," shouted Timmy as he paddled around on his new yellow boogie board.

Timmy loved coming to the beach every summer to visit his nana and grandpa. He looked forward to it all year. Sometimes his teacher would catch him daydreaming about it and have to remind him to pay attention. But he didn't care. In his mind he was on his magic board drifting away on the waves.

And that's exactly what he was doing--drifting away. He looked up and saw that he was much further out than he should be. He was beginning to feel scared, but the harder he paddled the further out the current carried him.

"Help, help," shouted Timmy, but he was too far from shore for anyone to hear. He knew his mother must be looking everywhere for him.

Just when Timmy had given up all hope of ever getting back, he felt a gentle bump against the board. He looked behind him but didn't see anything.

Suddenly, a large round head, with two big bulging eyes, popped out of the water and looked right at Timmy. Timmy's eyes grew just as big. Was this some sort of sea monster he had heard about in fairy tales?

“Wh-who are you,” Timmy stammered, “and wh-what are you?”

“I'm an octopus,” said the creature cheerfully.

“An oc-toe-puss?” asked Timmy, suddenly afraid.

“Yep, that's what I am. Have you never seen one of us before?” Timmy was too frightened to speak. He just sat there, wide-eyed, staring at this octopus.

“Well then,” said the octopus, “let me tell you a little about myself.” **(Song)**

Song: ***"REX, REX THE OCTOPUS"*** - CD Track 2

Hello, my name is Rex, and I'm an octopus
Though I'm a spineless creature, trust me I'm no wuss
If you're my friend I will not bite, but don't dare treat me bad
I'll shoot black ink all over you, that's what I do when I get mad

I'm Rex, Rex the octopus, an octopus that's me
Rex, Rex the octopus, my home's the deep blue sea

Ooh, I've got eight arms I think are really neat
Some people like to call them legs, but then where are my feet
I have a well-developed brain, still I can't read or spell
But when it comes to danger I can change my colors very well

I'm Rex, Rex the octopus, an octopus that's me
Rex, Rex the octopus, my home's the deep blue sea

I'll share a little secret, honest it's no lie
Lots of us are octopuses; we prefer it to oc-to-pi

To catch my food I get to use my unique mollusk charms
Like all these rows of suction cups stuck here on my arms
I stay away from moray eels cuz I'm their favorite snack
But if they take an arm or two, I just laugh & grow them back

I'm Rex, Rex the octopus, an octopus that's me
Rex, Rex the octopus, my home's the deep blue sea
I'm Rex, Rex the octopus, an octopus that's me
Rex, Rex the octopus, that's what I love to be.

"What's your name?" asked Rex.

"Timmy." Timmy began to calm down a little. This Rex seemed pretty friendly. Maybe he didn't need to be afraid of him after all.

"Well, Timmy, I think you need some help getting back to shore. Let me push you."

"Can you really do that?" asked Timmy hopefully.

"Sure," said Rex. "With these eight arms, I'll have you back before you can say 'octopus'." Rex puffed out his chest and proudly flexed the muscles in four of his arms. He liked showing them off, especially to his fish friends who didn't have any.

"Wow," exclaimed Timmy, "you must be really strong!"

Rex started pushing the boogie board toward shore. Before Timmy knew it he was back on the sand.

His mother ran over to hug him. “Promise me you'll never do that again,” she said sternly. “I was sick with worry.”

“I promise,” said Timmy, knowing he had done a silly thing.

“Good,” replied his mom. “Now go back to the cottage and change for dinner. Nana’s been cooking all afternoon.”

“OK,” said Timmy as his mom turned to leave. He wanted to tell his mother about Rex, but he wasn’t sure she would believe him. He’d wait until dinner when his grandpa was there. His grandpa would believe him; he always did.

Timmy looked for Rex to thank him for saving his life. He saw him lying on his back flapping his eight arms in the sand. He was trying to make a sand angel just like the two little girls next to him were doing.

Timmy laughed because Rex looked so funny waving his arms all around. Timmy walked over to him and helped him up. “Rex, how can I ever repay you for saving my life?”

“Ah, it was nothing,” said Rex shyly, swinging his number six arm back and forth in the sand.

“There must be *something*,” Timmy insisted.

Rex thought for a minute. “Well, I've never been on land before. Will you show me around?”

“Gosh, I don't know,” said Timmy. “Can you be out of the water all day? I mean, you might get sick or die or something.”

"Oh, I'll be fine, really, pleeease," begged Rex, even though his mother had warned him not to stay out too long.

"Well, OK," Timmy agreed. "I'll meet you here tomorrow morning at eight o'clock in front of this blue umbrella."

Rex was so excited. "How many more hours is that?" he asked.

"Sixteen," replied Timmy. "I know how to tell time."

"Oh, ok," said Rex scratching his head, not really sure he could count that high. He would have to ask his mother. He didn't want to be late for his special adventure. He couldn't wait to get back and tell all his friends. He scurried back to the water as he counted out loud on his arms. Timmy smiled remembering when he used to use his fingers to count. Then he turned and ran back to his grandparents' house to get ready for a roast chicken and mashed potatoes dinner, his favorite.

At the dinner table, Timmy got up the courage to tell his mom and grandparents about what really happened to him out in the ocean. "Rex saved my life; he pushed me all the way back to shore. I promised him I would take him all around town tomorrow."

"That sounds like a wonderful adventure," said Timmy's grandfather.

"Oh, I don't know," replied Timmy's mother. "Can Rex be out of the water all day?" She and Timmy's grandmother were very worried.

"I promise I'll look out for Rex very carefully. I won't let anything happen to him, honest," said Timmy. Timmy could hardly eat his dinner because he was so excited about the fun he and Rex were going to have. **(Song)**

Song: ***"TOMORROW IS THE DAY"*** (CD Track 4)

Tomorrow is the day that Rex will come to play
I'll show him all around the town
We'll stop and say hello to all the friends I know
And fall down laughing at the circus clowns

I'll take him to my secret cave, show him all the rocks I've saved
I'll teach him how to climb a tree
We'll go swinging in the park and before it gets too dark
Eat honey from a hive of honey bees

We'll march across some logs
And try to catch some frogs
We'll blast off in a rocket ship to Mars
We'll build castles in the sand
Everything will be so grand
Then we'll lie back in the grass
To count the stars

Yes, tomorrow is the day
That Rex will come to play
Together we will fly a kite
The wind will blow our hair
But we won't have a care
The sun will shine
Upon us big and bright

Tomorrow is the day
That Rex will come to play
It will be the best day of my life

The next morning, at exactly eight o'clock, Timmy met Rex on the beach in front of the blue umbrella. Rex was so happy to see Timmy that he waved all eight arms at one time. He lost his balance and fell over onto the sand.

Timmy burst out laughing. "Here, give me your arm."

"Which one?" teased Rex, not moving to get up.

"Oh, how about number three," replied Timmy, playing along with Rex. "In

fact, give me your five, a high-five."

"A high what?" asked Rex, as he stood up.

"A high-five, you know, like this." Timmy showed Rex how to high-five. Rex put five arms up at the same time and almost fell onto the sand again. He flapped his arms wildly to keep from falling. "You only need one arm at a time," laughed Timmy. Rex quickly learned to do a perfect high-five.

"Wait 'til my friends see this," said Rex eagerly, as he continued to do high-fives in the air.

“Come on, “ said Timmy, “I'm hungry. Let's go to the bakery and get a sticky bun.”

“Yeah,” replied Rex excitedly, wanting to do everything that Timmy did, although he had no idea what a sticky bun was.

As they got closer to town, they walked by a small outdoor market where vendors were selling fruits and vegetables and fresh fish. “What are these?”

asked Rex, fascinated by all the brightly colored shapes.

“The red ones are tomatoes, the yellow ones are corn, and the blue ones are blueberries,” explained Timmy.

“Would you boys like to try some blueberries?” offered the kind woman at the fruit stand.

“Sure, thanks,” said Timmy as he put a few berries in his mouth. After a few seconds, he playfully turned to Rex. “Hey Rex, look!” Timmy started jumping around and showing off his blue tongue to Rex.

" I want a blue tongue too!" clamored Rex. The vendor smiled and gave Rex some berries to eat. Soon his tongue was blue too. Timmy and Rex ran around trying to see whose tongue was bluer. Rex couldn't believe how much fun there was on land.

At the end of the row, old Mr. Cutter, the fishmonger, stepped out from behind his cart and yelled, “Stop, sonny boy. How much do you want for that octopus? It looks like a *reeeal* tasty one to me.”

“He's not for sale; he's my friend.” Timmy was trying to sound brave.

“Come, come, now lad, what do you want with a stupid octopus? I'll give ya fifty dollars fer that critter. Fifty dollars will buy ya a shiny new scooter.” Mr. Cutter took out a fifty-dollar bill and waved it in front of Timmy.

Timmy wanted a new scooter very badly. He'd never had fifty dollars before. He looked down at Rex. Rex looked up at Timmy with tears in his eyes. Timmy knew he could never sell his friend for anything, not even fifty dollars. He knew *he* wouldn't want to be sold for fifty dollars.

Rex began to shake with fear. His mother had warned him that there were dangers on land. "I don't want to be sold to some old fishmonger," whimpered Rex. "Oh, how I wish I were back in my cozy den at the bottom of the sea." **(Song)**

Song: ***"IF I'M NOT CAREFUL"*** (CD Track 6)

If I'm not careful, I'll become dinner in some fine restaurant
Who ever thought an octopus would be something they want
There're lots of us critters in the sea
So who would miss just one
I, I would sure miss me
If I were at the bottom of somebody's tum tum
Tum tum tum tum tum

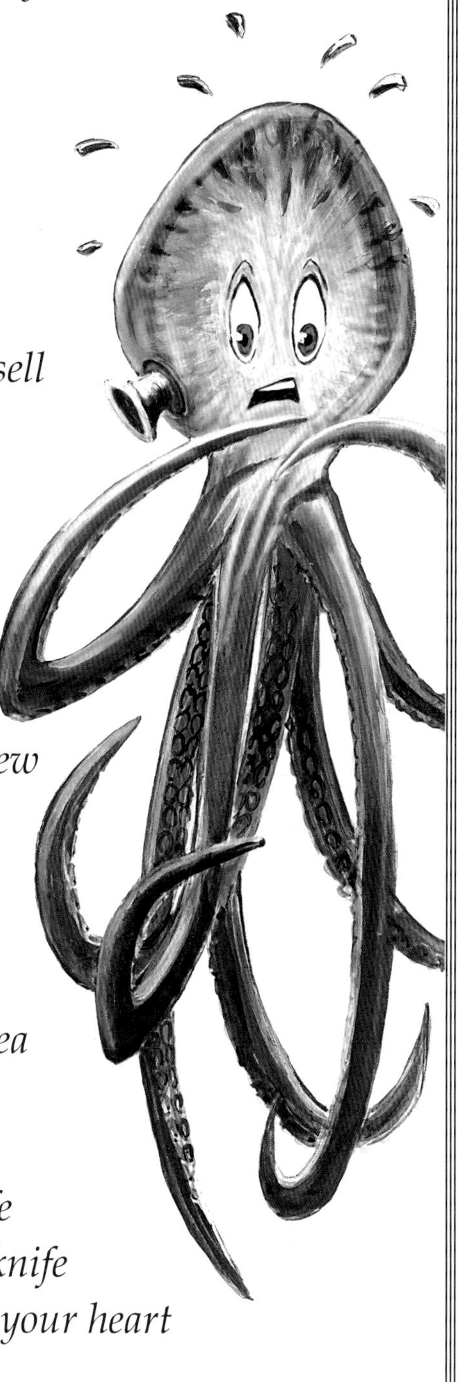

If I'm not careful, ol' Mr. Cutter will slice me up to sell
Who will buy which part of me, only time will tell
So, run, run, run real fast, run for your dear life
Don't, don't, don't get caught
By some fishmonger's knife
By some fishmonger's knife

If I'm not careful, I'll be cut up in pieces for some stew
You'll find me on a menu under octopus fondue
No, no I won't go, I have to get away
I was born to be much more than special of the day

If I'm not careful, I'll never play again beneath the sea
I'll never be more than a twig upon our family tree

If I'm not careful, today will be the last day of my life
I never thought that it would end by one swipe of a knife
Please, Mr. Cutter, please oh please, please find it in your heart
To keep this little octopus intact with all his parts
Intact with all his parts

If I'm not careful, I'll become dinner in some fine rest-au-rant.

The sound of Mr. Cutter smacking his lips made Timmy jump. Rex was trembling all over; each of his eight arms was shaking very badly. Timmy knew he had to do something fast. "Grab my hand," he yelled to Rex. Rex wrapped his number one and two arms around Timmy's hand and away they ran, Rex flying out like a kite behind Timmy.

Mr. Cutter was chasing after them waving his butcher knife. They could

hear his big, flat feet thumping right behind them.

"Hurry," shouted Rex.

Rex was getting heavy, and it was hard for Timmy to run very fast, but he knew he had to save his friend. "Hang on Rex!" Timmy yelled. With one last burst of energy, Timmy dashed across the field, and they got away from the wicked fishmonger just in time.

"Whew, that was close," panted Timmy, trying to catch his breath. Rex looked as if he had seen a ghost; his eyes were popping out of his head. He had never been so frightened in his entire life.

"Th, th-thanks," said Rex still trembling. "Looks like *you* saved *my* life this time."

"It was no big deal," said Timmy, but secretly he was proud that he had rescued his friend from such an awful fate. "Come on, I'm really hungry now. Let's get those sticky buns."

Timmy and Rex sat outside of Auntie B's Bakery eating their sticky buns.

Rex's number one and two arms got so covered with sticky bun that they almost stuck together. He had a great time licking them off. "This is fun. Nothing ever sticks to my arms under the water." Timmy laughed.

Just as they finished their last bite of sticky buns, Timmy saw two girls coming toward them. One was pushing the other in a wheelchair. They both had long brown hair and big brown eyes. "Oh, here come Maria and her sister, Ana," said Timmy happily. "They're friends of mine. They can speak Spanish."

"Spanish?" asked Rex.

"It's a language," answered Timmy. "Their parents are from Mexico. I study it in school. I can say 'my name is Timmy' in Spanish: me llamo Timmy."

"How do you say *my* name in Spanish?" Rex wanted to know.

"Me llamo Rex," replied Timmy.

"Me llamo Rex, me llamo Rex, me llamo Rex. Wow, I can speak Spanish!" Rex was very proud of himself.

"What's that?" asked Rex, pointing to the wheelchair. He was full of questions, but there were so many things to learn.

"It's a wheelchair," said Timmy. "It's for people who can't walk, like Ana."

"Why can't she walk?" Rex wanted to know.

"Because she was hurt in an accident and is paralyzed. Her legs don't work anymore."

"I could give her two of mine," offered Rex. "I can grow them back, you

know," he said with pride.

"Well, that's very kind of you," said Timmy, "but you don't have legs, you have arms."

"Oh, yeah," said Rex sadly. He really wanted to give Ana two of his arms.

Just then the girls came up to their table. "Hi Ana. Hi Maria," said Timmy.

"Hola," both girls replied. "Who's your friend?" Ana looked at Rex and smiled.

Rex thought Ana and Maria were very pretty. He started turning several shades of red. He didn't know what was happening to him. He tried to hide behind Timmy. "This is Rex," said Timmy. "He's an octopus. Rex, say hi to Ana and Maria."

Rex peeked out from behind Timmy just long enough to say, 'hi.' **(Song)**

Song: *"BLUSHING"* (CD Track 8)

What's happening to me, I wonder
I've never felt like this before
My skin is turning red all over
In my ears I hear the ocean roar

This feeling I'm feeling's so different
It feels silly and warm and good
I've only heard about it in stories
Until now I never understood

Could it be I'm blushing
The blood is rushing to my face
By gosh by golly gee I'm blushing
It's like I'm part of the human race

A pretty girl is smiling at me
I wonder what I should do now
If only I were Prince Charming
I would have figured it out somehow

I'm starting to like this feeling
I hope it never goes away
I swear my head is reeling
And my heart is coming out to play

Could it be I'm blushing
The blood is rushing to my face
By gosh by golly gee I'm blushing
It's like I'm part of the human race

“I have a stuffed animal on my bed that looks a lot like you,” Ana said to Rex. “His name is Archie. You should come over and meet him.”

“Yeah,” that's a great idea,” agreed Maria. “Let’s all go to our house and play.”

Rex was really excited and started skipping behind Timmy and the girls. He was enjoying his adventure on land but knew he had to get back to the water soon; after all, he was an octopus, and he would dry up and die if he stayed out too long. Besides, his mom and dad would really miss him.

By the time they got to Ana and Maria’s house they were all the best of friends. Maria fixed lemonade for everone, and Ana introduced Rex to Archie. “Hey, Archie, gimme five,” Rex giggled as he pretended to teach Archie to high-five.

They taught Rex how to play *Go Fish*. Rex had trouble holding the cards; every time he tried to shuffle them they went flying all over the room, causing Maria, Ana, and Timmy to shriek with laughter. And whenever one of them asked Rex for a card, instead of saying, "go fish," Rex would shout,

"go octopus" and burst out laughing. He thought it was very funny.

They spent the afternoon playing hide-and-seek, Simon Says, and Tic-Tac-Toe. "I know a game we can play," said Ana with a mischievous look in her eyes.

"What is it?" asked Timmy.

"Musical Chairs," replied Ana quite smugly, spinning her chair around.

"No way,"declared Timmy and Maria; "you always win." They knew that Ana loved to play musical chairs because she never lost; she always had a chair. Everyone was having a grand time.

Suddenly, Rex started to choke and gasp for air. He put two of his arms up to his throat. "I think- I better-get back-to the water," he said, trying desperately to breathe. He knew he was in trouble. Oh, why hadn't he listened to his mother? She would never let him have another adventure on land. The room seemed to be spinning, and he was starting to feel dizzy. Then he fell to the floor.

Maria rushed over to Rex and put her ear to his chest. "He's still breathing," she said.

Timmy slapped Rex lightly across his face. "Rex, Rex, open your eyes," but he didn't respond.

"Oh, what are we going to do?" cried Ana. "How will we get him back to the water?"

Timmy shook his head. "If only we had a bicycle or a scooter or *something*, we could get him to the water so much faster."

Then, at the exact same moment, Timmy, Ana, and Maria all turned to each other and shouted, "The wheelchair!"

Timmy and Maria picked up Rex and put him on Ana's lap. "Hold on to him," Timmy said to Ana. Then he and Maria ran to the wheelchair and started pushing with all their might.

"Come on," urged Maria, "we have to hurry. Vámonos!" They all rushed from the room, Maria and Timmy running and pushing the wheelchair.

Rex looked like a rag doll draped over Ana's lap. He could hardly breathe. He began to mumble: "Where's the ocean? I need water. Help."

The wheelchair was rolling and bumping over the rough sidewalk. "He's starting to slide off," yelled Ana, trying to hold onto Rex with all her might. "Hurry!"

"Hang on Rex!"urged Timmy, "we're almost there!"

Finally, Rex felt the wheelchair being pushed across the sand. Timmy and Maria lifted Rex off Ana's lap and set him down in the shallow water.

"Keep splashing water over him," shouted Timmy. Maria frantically splashed water on Rex with one hand and held one of his arms with the other. She was about to cry.

Ana took off the locket she was wearing, leaned over, and slipped it around Rex's neck. "This is my lucky charm," she whispered; "it *always* works." **(Song)**

Song: ***"REX OH REX"*** (CD Track 10)

Rex, oh Rex, what have you done
Come back to us little friend
If you should die we surely would cry
It's too soon to be the end

Rex, oh Rex, don't leave us now
Hang on with all your might
Soon we will be at the edge of the sea
And everything will be all right

Rex, oh Rex, we hope you can hear all the prayers in our hearts
God is above sending down his pure love, have faith that he's doing his part

Rex, oh Rex, we're almost there, please wear this special charm
This time next year we'll be standing right here to welcome you back in our arms

Rex, oh Rex, don't leave us now, hang on with all your might
Soon we will be at the edge of the sea, and everything will be all right

"Look," said Maria joyfully, "I think I see his chest moving up and down a little."

Rex's eyes fluttered open. In a few moments he was breathing normally again. He sat up but was still a little dizzy. He tried to stand but had trouble keeping his balance. Finally, with Timmy and Maria each holding on to an arm, Rex was able to stand. They all cheered and sighed with relief. Rex was trying to hold back his tears. It was the second close call he'd had in one day.

He turned to his three friends. "How can I ever thank you for saving my life? I guess the ocean's a safer place for me."

Maria gave Rex a kiss on the cheek. "Come back and play with us sometime. We promise we'll be more careful."

"I'd like that," said Rex, blinking his eyes and touching his cheek where Maria had kissed him. Then he looked down and noticed the silver locket around his neck. He looked up and saw Ana smiling at him. "Your wheelchair saved my life; you're my hero."

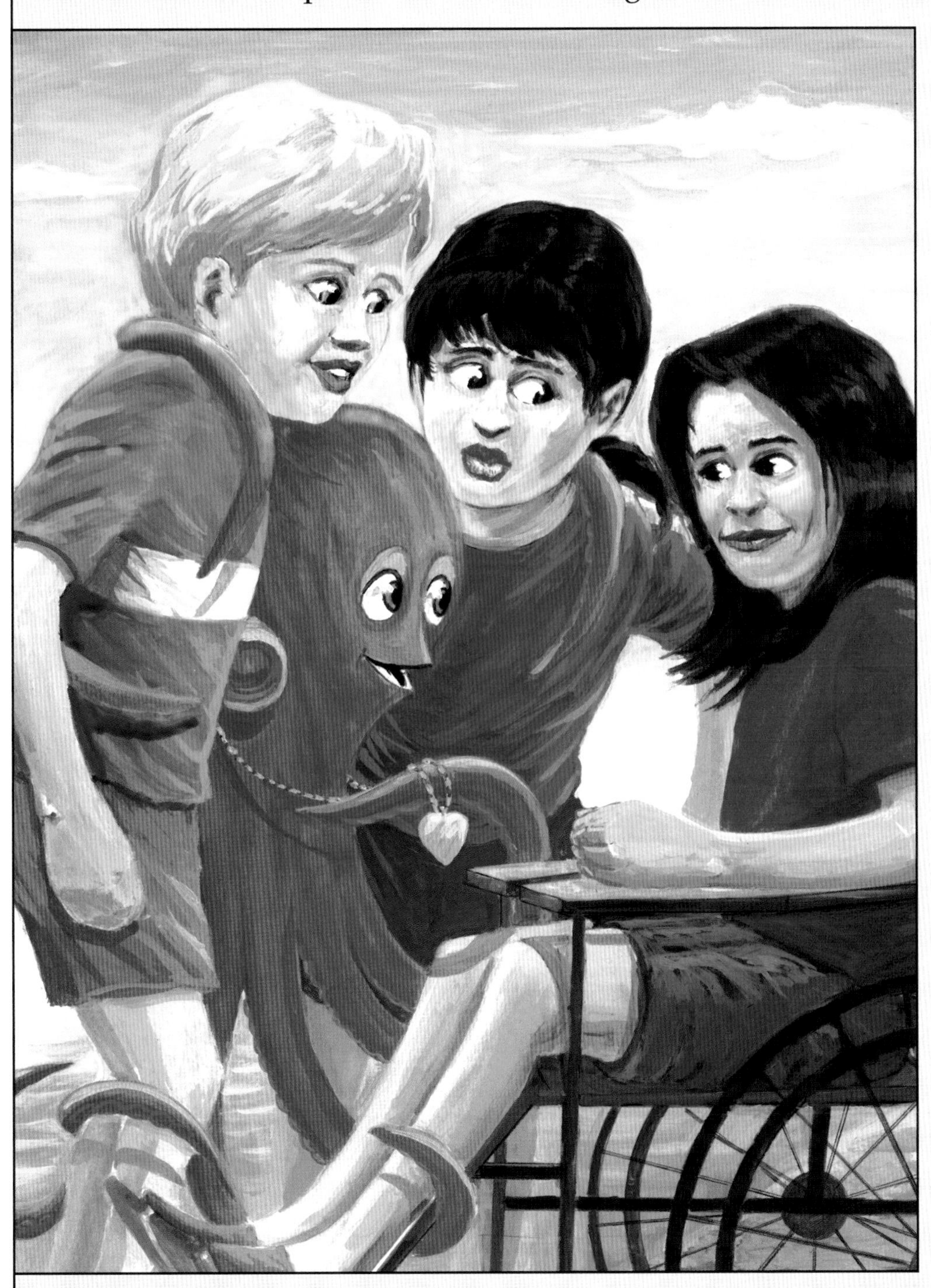

Now it was Ana's turn to blush. She never dreamed that she would be anyone's hero. "We'll miss you," she said softly.

"Hurry now," urged Timmy trying to sound grown-up. "You better get back home."

Rex looked up at his friend. "Will I ever see you again?"

"You bet," said Timmy, "next summer. I'm counting on you to push me back to shore again."

"Yeah, and I'll be counting on *you* to save me from that wicked old Mr. Cutter," replied Rex. Timmy and Rex both laughed and gave each other a high-five. **(Song)**

Song: *"COUNT ON ME"* (CD Track 12)

(Rex)
One, two, three, count on me, I'm your friend from the deep blue sea
Small but mighty, yes sir-ee, one, two, three, you can count on me

(Timmy)
One, two, three, count on me, I'm your friend and I'll always be
Cross my heart and slap my knee, one, two, three, you can count on me

(Rex & Timmy)
One, two, three, four, five, we'll be friends all through our lives
Six, seven, eight, nine, ten, makes no difference where or when

One, two, three, count on me, just like brothers we will be
Tweedle-dum and Tweedle-dee, one, two, three, you can count on me

(Ana & Maria)
Uno, dos, tres, y más, conmigo siempre contarás
Te amo y me amas, uno, dos, tres, y más

(Timmy, Ana, & Maria)
One, two, three, count on me, we're your friends and we'll always be
We like you and you like we, one, two, three, you can count on me

(Everyone)
One, two, three, four, five, we'll be friends all through our lives
Six, seven, eight, nine, ten, let's all sing this song again

(Timmy, Ana, & Maria)
One, two, three, count on me, we're your friends and we'll always be
We like you and you like we, one, two, three, you can count on me
I like you and you like me,
Cross my heart and slap my knee
One, two, three, you can count…on….me.

Rex waved goodbye to Ana, Maria, and Timmy, then turned and walked deeper into the ocean. As he disappeared beneath the sea, Timmy, Ana, and Maria all shouted and waved goodbye back, sad but happy they had made such a wonderful new friend and excited about the new adventure they would have next year!

No octopuses were harmed in the making of this book.